Elephantastic!

by Michael Engler

Illustrated by Joëlle Tourlonias

Peter Pauper Press, Inc.
White Plains, New York

"Andrew, I'm going out onto the balcony," called Mommy.
"Can you take the package in the hallway to our neighbors upstairs?"

"Sure," said Andrew, but he wasn't really listening.

He was busy drawing a treasure map,
which was much more important.
It could come in handy some day.

It wasn't until he finished the map that he remembered Mommy had asked him to do something. But what had it been?

"Mommy?" he called out, and went into the hallway.

When he got there he discovered a huge box.

"A package?" he thought. "It must be for me! So *that's* what Mommy said."

Andrew lifted the package. It wasn't heavy at all.

"What could be inside?" he wondered. Carefully, he began to open the box.

"An elephant!" he cried.

Sure enough, a big gray stuffed elephant popped its head out of the box. Andrew had always wanted one just like it.

"Hello," said the elephant. "My name is Timbo."

A talking elephant! Andrew could hardly believe his luck. He carried Timbo to his room, then he ran to the kitchen to get lemonade and cookies. He sat down on the bed and asked Timbo to tell him all about his adventures in Africa.

The elephant closed his eyes and began.

He told of savannahs and deserts so huge that only elephants could cross them, of jungles so dark and deep that only elephants dared to venture into them.

He told of snowcapped Mount Kilimanjaro, so high only elephants could climb it. He told of lions roaring at dusk, a sound that struck fear into all the animals— all except for the elephants.

Andrew listened so closely that his heart began to beat faster and faster. He could hardly stand it—it was time for him to have those kinds of adventures, too.

And so Andrew and Timbo climbed to the top
of Mount Kilimanjaro.

They scrambled and clambered to catch their breaths.
"It's so windy up here!" shouted Andrew.

Then they tumbled down into the sun-parched valley belo[w]
and danced a lively rain dance.

They skipped and jumped and spun around.
"This is fun!" Andrew said.

Next, they traveled to where the wild lions lived.

They tiptoed and lurked and scurried by.
"How exciting!" whispered Andrew.

They hiked through vast savannahs and into the dense dark jungle.

They crawled and crept and swung.

Andrew looked into the wild forest beyond and thought, "This is elephantastic!"

Suddenly Andrew heard a voice.
"What are you doing under the bed?" asked Mommy.

"I'm playing with the elephant from the package! He can talk!" said Andrew.

"Oh no!" sighed his mommy. "That package was delivered for Louise."

"But I thought it was for me!" cried Andrew.

"I'm afraid not. Come on . . . let's bring it to her together."

The climb upstairs had never felt harder.

Andrew squeezed Timbo tight. He followed his
mommy reluctantly, step by step.

At the top of the stairs he rang the bell and hoped
no one would answer. But he heard footsteps anyway.
A moment later Louise opened the door.

"Hello, Andrew," she said.

Before Andrew could say anything, Louise saw the box
and the stuffed animal in his hands.

"At last! My birthday present from Grandma and Grandpa
is here!" she exclaimed, taking Timbo from Andrew.

Andrew turned quickly and ran down the stairs,
his eyes filling with tears.

At dinner Andrew was very quiet. Teardrops fell onto his slice of buttered bread.

"Oh, sweetheart," said Mommy softly. "It's only a stuffed elephant."

"It's NOT just a stuffed elephant! His name is Timbo and he talked to me!" sniffled Andrew.

Mommy shook her head. "But Andrew, stuffed animals can't . . . "

Just then the doorbell rang.

It was Louise, with Timbo in her arms. She held the elephant up to Andrew and whispered, "Timbo says he misses you."

Andrew's heart leapt. He hugged Timbo as tightly as he could.
Then he looked at Louise and asked, "Do you want to go on an adventure?"

Louise smiled and said, "That would be elephantastic!"

For my Mama
— Joëlle Tourlonias

Published by Peter Pauper Press, Inc.
202 Mamaroneck Avenue
White Plains, New York 10601
U.S.A.

Published in the United Kingdom and Europe by Peter Pauper Press, Inc.
c/o White Pebble International
Unit 2, Plot 11 Terminus Rd.
Chichester, West Sussex PO19 8TX, UK

Library of Congress Cataloging-in-Publication Data

Engler, Michael, 1961–
[Elefantastisch. English]
Elephantastic! / by Michael Engler ; illustrated by Joelle Tourlonias.
pages cm
Originally published in German by Annette Betz Verlag in 2014 under title: Elefantastisch.
Summary: "Andrew finds a mysterious box in his hallway with a talking stuffed elephant inside!
The two friends set off on an adventure. It's a wonderful afternoon--until Mommy interrupts.
It turns out the box was meant for someone else"-- Provided by publisher.
ISBN 978-1-4413-0841-2 (hardcover : alk. paper) [1. Toys--Fiction. 2. Elephants--Fiction.]
I. Tourlonias, Joelle, illustrator. II. Title.
PZ7.1.E54El 2015
[E]--dc23
2014029029

ISBN 978-1-4413-0841-2
Manufactured for Peter Pauper Press, Inc.
Printed in Hong Kong

7 6 5 4 3 2 1

Visit us at www.peterpauper.com